ColorQuest Collections

Fun and creative coloring books

Calming | Relaxing | Stress Relief

For more fun and creative coloring books, search for ColorQuest Collections in your favorite bookstore!

Thank You

PLEASE LEAVE US A REVIEW!

IF YOU ENJOYED THIS COLORING BOOK, PLEASE TAKE A MOMENT TO LEAVE A REVIEW. YOUR FEEDBACK HELPS US IMPROVE AND GUIDES OTHER CREATIVE SPIRITS TO THEIR PERFECT COLORING ADVENTURE!

SCAN HERE

FOR MORE CREATIVE COLORING BOOKS, PLEASE SEARCH FOR COLORQUEST COLLECTIONS IN YOUR FAVORITE BOOKSTORE!

COLORQUEST COLLECTIONS

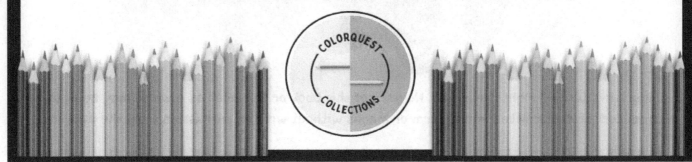

Made in the USA
Coppell, TX
04 December 2024

41750668R00057